I0618099

"THE QUEEN, THE MOON, AND THE MOUNTAIN"

Victoria Denee

Copyright © 2025 Victoria
Denee

All rights reserved·

ISBN:979-8-89397-440-9

DEDICATION

I dedicate this book to my daughter, Nyiema Allure. She is every star in

the sky...and the moon too. May you live a life that doesn't require you

to dim your light. I love you SugaBoo

ACKNOWLEDGMENTS

Thank you to my mother Darlean, who has loved me unconditionally. Thank you to my Godfather and pastor Bishop Ronald Johnson, for choosing me and pouring into my gifts. Thank you to my son Nasir Messiah, for being pure love and joy, may your heart stay fearless forever. Thank you to my sisters Marsha and Jessica, you are amazing women and mothers and help me to be better daily. Thank you to my favorite, my Aunt Deanie, she has always seen me the real me and loved me anyway. (Auntie, I miss him too, but I think this book would make him smile).

Many moons ago, in the land where the Earth held hands with the sky, there was a queen, and her name was Ifede. Queen Ifede was loving, wise, and she ruled with fairness and justice. Queen Ifede didn't just have a beautiful heart, she herself was also exceedingly beautiful. Her lovely cocoa brown skin sparkled with flecks of gold as she weaved baskets with her maidens by the river. Her hair looked like a mane and halo when she emerged from her ile odi wearing her crown. And her eyes, they shined like precious diamonds.

In the heat of each day Queen Ifede would go walking among the Mopane trees and talk to them. She would sit beneath those trees and tell them stories until the Sun would begin to take his rest, and on her way home she would sing with the birds, serenading the sky. She loved her village and her village loved her back. At night she would dance with the children and young women around the fire as the men played the djembe.

Though Ifede seemed to always be surrounded by friends and subjects, she had no family of her own. Her father and mother had already moved on to the place of the Ancestors. Even on the loveliest of days, the shinning of the Sun was nothing to be compared to her mother's smile. And even under her favorite Mopane tree Ifede still had known no presence more comforting than her fathers'. Nights in her ile odi were long and lonely, so she would go up to the high place where the Earth touched sky and stare at the stars until she fell asleep. She did this for many years, so many in fact, that she even had a favorite star. She called this star Aiyana which means eternal blooming flower.

One night, she walked up to the high place and called out to Mother Moon saying;

"Beloved Mama Osupa, thank you for lending your glow to light our way in the darkness of night. How lovely you are surrounded by the stars, your many children! I have this heart full of love and no one of my own to give it to! There's no one to greet me in my ile odi after a long day in the village, no one to tell my secrets too, no one to fill in the emptiness of my heart. Although I sing and dance I am very lonely."

At that moment Mother Moon opened Her eyes and set them on Ifede, enveloping her in a cool shimmering light. Then Mother Moon began to speak, "Omo, why is your heart heavy? You have the trees to talk to, and the birds to sing with, and the people of your village to dance and play music. I have put a star just for you in the sky and she keeps you company at night."

Ifede was taken off guard by Mother Moon's voice, which sounded like the ocean, and she didn't want to seem ungrateful. With great care she replied; "Yes ma'am that is true. But the trees cannot talk back to me, and the birds don't sing familiar songs, and people of my village have families of their own to love, and I love Aiyana but it is such a long walk each night to see her and then she goes away when Father Sun rises and I am alone again."

Mama Osupa said, "Yes I suppose you are right. What would you like for me to do?".

Excited that Mother Moon offered to help her, Ifede said "Mama Osupa, you have so many children I couldn't even count them. Could you give me a star of my own?"

Mother Moon was quiet, reasoning with herself. After a few moments Mother Moon agreed to give her Aiyana, her favorite star.

Queen Ifede, overjoyed, began to cry. She said, "E Dupe Mama Osupa! you've given me a great gift, I can't thank you enough!".

Mama Osupa said, "E kabo omo, but I must tell you that what you have asked is no small thing. Aiyana is yours, but you must pluck her from the sky yourself. The things that we love most are not simply given they are earned. You must take the journey to see Baba Atijo Oke (Father Old Mountain), ask him if you can stand on his shoulders so that you will be up high enough to reach out and get her. But when you go to him to ask, don't show up empty handed. For in this world we get nothing for nothing."

Queen Ifede listened eagerly, then she replied, "But what can I give Baba Atijo Oke?"

Mama Osupa, "Eh-eh, you must come up with that yourself. Gifts are given from our own hearts. You have three days to get Aiyana before the New Moon and I close my arms so that you cannot take her. Move with haste, but act in wisdom ife mi."

Then Mama Osupa smiled and closed her eyes.

The next day Queen Ifede rose from her bed filled with joy and anticipation for the journey she was about to embark on. She searched all over her ile ode for a gift to offer Baba Atijo Oke, first she decided on giving him one of her favorite books thinking he must get bored standing in one place all the time. A book would be a lovely distraction. Then she thought, I will give him my Mother's crown. The lovely gold crown had three glowing emeralds on its front and a dazzling moon stone on the back. It was uniquely beautiful and one of a kind. Surely Baba Atijo Oke would enjoy having something so beautiful and valuable to look at. Lastly, Ifede thought, I will give him my Baba's drum. It is the finest djembe that had ever been made when struck it almost seemed to speak. Yebo, Baba Atijo Oke will love these gifts!

She gathered some food in a satchel to take on her journey, she placed her favorite book on the top of the bag and tied it closed. Then Ifede shined up her Mama's crown and placed it on her head, finally she strapped the djembe to her back and set out to see Baba Atijo Oke.

As Ifede was walking she began thinking to herself, Father Sun has never shined this brightly before. Sweat was dripping down her lovely face, and her hair was very hot on her neck and back. She came up to a clearing among the trees, and saw the banks of the rushing river. At that moment she remembered, in her haste, she forgot to pack water to drink. The cool blue of the water rushing before her seemed to only intensify her thirst. She approached the river and said, "Kind Odo, would it be alright if I came down and got a drink from your waters?"

At that moment a wave stood up tall as a Mopan Tree in front of her and said, "Yeeeesss child, on this hot day my cool waters are just what you need to help with the heat!"

Relieved that the odo was so kind, Ifede began to stoop down to get a drink.

"Wait, wait, wait! What do you have for me in return for the gift of my water? The Odo asked.

Ifede replied, "I don't have anything to give you kind Odo, I am on my way to see Baba

Atijo Oke to ask if I can stand on his shoulders and all that I have is for him."

The Odo's waters began to laugh, then she said, "Well, ife mi, in this life you get nothing for nothing. What about that fine djembe on your back, surely you can give that to me! Out there all alone there is no one to play it for Baba. But there are many villages along my banks, and one of my children will play it for me every day." All of a sudden, the waters of the odo swelled and a wave came up and snatched the djembe from Ifede's back.

Ifede stood stunned at what just happened, then a full wine skin washed up next to her and the Odo said, "Fair is fair, now take what you need

and go."

Ifede picked up the full wine skin and trudged away. Feeling sad and angry, she stopped for the night beneath the nearby trees and took her rest.

The next rising Ifede thought to herself, I may have lost Baba's drum but I still have my book and Mama's crown to offer Baba Atijo Oke so I must continue. And continue she did, following the walkway by the river until she came to a fork in the path. At that moment Ifede remembered that in her haste she forgot to bring a map. Ifede stood at the fork in her path for a very long time trying to figure out which way to go. Finally, a grey hooded vulture perched on the tree just beside her and said,

"My God, this girl has forgotten how to walk! What a silly thing to do right in the middle of your journey! Picking up your feet is so easy, eh!"

Ifede answered and said, "No Igbin, I haven't forgotten how to walk! I'm trying to go see Baba Atijo Oke and I don't know which way to go."

To which the vulture snidely responded, "Well then you must have forgotten how to read, just look at your map silly girl!"

"I would but I left my map at home." Ifede whined.

"Mmmhh, a difficult situation indeed. If only there was a kind bird that could see farther down the way than you can to help guide you on your way...oh wait. I am a bird and it just so happens that I live not too far from Baba,I could show you the way."

Ifede, who had tears welling up in her honey brown eyes, looked up to the bird and said, "Oh Igbin, could you please show me the way! I only have one more day to get there and without you I will definitely get lost. Please, please help me.

The vulture looking down at Ifede, tilted his head and said, "Well silly girl in this life you get no-thing for nothing. Give that lovely crown and I will show you the way."

"But this crown is a gift for Baba because I must ask him if I may stand on his shoulders." Ifede said.

"Well the shine of that crown is what caught my eye and brought me down to you in the first place so that is what I want. You give it to me and I will lead you, that is my offer. Take it or leave it, or in your case, take it or stand here!"

Ifede thought to herself, I've already lost most of this day and if I'm going to get Aiyana I must get to Baba. I still have my book to offer him, so it seems I have no choice.

Ifede looked up at the bird and said, "Igbin if you will lead me to Baba Atijo Oke and safely back to my village I will give you my crown."

Before the words finished leaving her mouth the bird swooped down and grabbed the crown from her head and said, "Wonderful, now silly girl, follow me."

As she followed Igbin, Father Sun began to set and the evening started to grow cold. Very cold. Ifede was shuttering with every step she took. Igbin noticing how she had begun to tremble said, "I don't suppose you remembered to bring a blanket or anything to start a fire huh...silly girl"

Ifede just quietly continued to walk, she had come too far to let her haste or the searing wit of a mean bird stop her. At that moment Ifede could see the orange glow of a fire and hear the singing of an elderly woman up ahead of her. Relieved at the idea that there was a sweet old soul just ahead, Ifede increased her pace. As she approached, she was greeted by the older woman who was seated on a log by the fire

mending her small fishing net.
Without looking up the woman
said, "Well well Queen Ifede!
You've wandered a long way
from the village! What are you
doing out here?"

"Bawo beloved, I'm on my way to see Baba Atijo Oke. The journey has been a lot more difficult than I anticipated though."

The woman said, "Yes my love, the most rewarding journeys always tend to be harder than we think they will be. Come over and sit down, warm yourself by the fire, and get one of those fish I roasted and have something to eat."

Queen Ifede, taken aback by the generosity of this stranger continued to stand there looking on for a moment until the caw of her guide Igbin, who had been circling above them, jolted her into movement. Ifede walked over to the fire and sat on the ground with her back resting against the log, she grabbed one of the fish on the wooden platter in front of her. As she began to eat, the words of Osupa played in her mind, "in this life you get nothing for nothing."

Right then the woman broke the silence and said, "Yes ma'am that is right, and that book in your bag will do quite nicely."

Ifede with wide eyes turned to look at the woman, "how do you know I have a book in my satchel and how did you know what I was thinking?"

"Well Mama Osupa loves sending her children on journey's and here you are, but she always sends them with some of her wisdom too."

Ifede, exhausted and hungry and cold took no time to hesitate, she reached into her bag, took out the book and handed it to the woman who received it with a big smile. The two sat by the fire and talked and ate, then finally, went to sleep.

The next day when Ifede rose from her sleep, she looked around and the woman was gone. The fire was gone and so was the log the woman was sitting on. Ifede stood up and looked around confused as to where the woman could have gone, surely she didn't just disappear. Then ifede looked at the ground where she had laid her head and noticed that there was a small pouch tied closed laying there. The queen picked up the pouch and saw a note had been tied to it as well, the note read; Move with haste, but act with wisdom.

A gift for Baba Atijo Oke.

Queen Ifede's mouth dropped open and she began to shake her head in disbelief. Who was this woman, why was she so kind, how did she know about the book...

Just as her thoughts began to run away with various flights of fancy, Igbin swooped down and said, "Are we going to see Baba or are you just going keep standing there silly girl?"

Queen Ifede had begun to get used to the way that her feathery guide spoke so she no longer took offense with his favorite thing to call her, silly girl. "Hush now, bird and lead the way."

Ifede put the pouch in her bag and walked on. They hadn't been on the path long before

Ifede could feel the ground vibrating, and a low deep voice began to wrap around her.

"That is him, Baba Atijo Oke. He's usually quiet but every now and then he gets lonesome so he moans."

Ifede thought to herself, I understand that feeling. Maybe I've been nervous for no reason. Baba must surely understand why I'm making this journey and why I have to ask him to help me.

Their path grew narrow, the grass gave way to dirt, and that dirt eventually became gravel. All the while the ground continued to vibrate beneath her feet, it was as if she could feel him breathing. Igbin yelled from just above her head, well I have fulfilled the first part of

my promise I will take this crown to my nest and come back to take you home. Then he cawed and flew away.

Standing alone at the face of this great mountain Ifede felt small and even more nervous than before. Baba Atijo Oke was too vast for her to comprehend; she couldn't even tell where he began and ended. Then the mountain in front of her moaned a loud sad moan and opened his eyes.

"You didn't follow rude Igbin all this way to just stand there astonished, how can I help you?" Baba said.

Ifede's voice and body shaking she said, "Bawo Baba Atijo Oke, I'm sorry to bother you. My name is Queen Ifede. Mama Osupa sent me here to ask if I can stand on your shoulders so that I may get my star from the sky."

"Stand on my shoulders, why should I let you? The last time I let someone stand on my shoulders they took my favorite star and never came back. You see Osupa is their Mama but I am their Baba, my lovely star would sing with me and I never felt alone."

It had never occurred to Ifede that Baba Atijo Oke would have some relation to the stars, or that he may say no to her request.

Baba continued, "Even now you stand ready to ask of me, but then you will leave. Having what you want, I will be all alone again. Not only that but you have come empty handed!"

Ifede quickly began rummaging through her bag to get the pouch the old woman had left her, "No Baba I haven't come empty handed, I brought this for you." As she pulled the pouch from her bag whatever was inside began to sing.

Baba Atijo Oke's eyes widened as he said, "Oh ife mi is that you! Queen Ifede you have brought back my favorite star!" Right then the pouch fell open and a beautiful glowing orb of light emerged. Shining with a diamond like brilliance the star sang out loud and lovely as it began to ascend the mountain and rest in the sky.

"What beautiful heart you must have to bring back my star so that I am not lonely, I will grant your request! Climb up to my shoulder and reach

out your hand."

Ifede very carefully began to scale the face of the mountain, up, up, up she climbed until she had the clouds tangled in hair. She was standing face to face with her Aiyona. Ifede said, "Bawo Aiyana I am Queen Ifede and I have come to take you with me."

Aiyana, the queen's star said, "Yebo Mama, I watched your long journey to come get me. You must tell me about your adventure!"

Ifede reached out her hand and the star laid itself in the queen's palm. Her gental glow warmed Ifede's face and hands. Tears that had before been so full of sorrow, were now overflowing with joy. For you see, Queen Ifede's heart finally understood why it longed so much for Aiyana; it was never her company but always her peace that made Queen Ifede love her so much. This peace she had journeyed so far to get was finally within reach, and she knew in that moment that she would never have to be without it again.

ABOUT THE AUTHOR

Victoria Denee is an author and performer based in Indianapolis, IN, originally from Poplar Bluff, Missouri. A lifelong writer and entertainer, she began her stage career at just 13 years old. While poetry had always been a part of her journey, the birth of her children deepened her passion for storytelling. She sought to use her gifts in writing and communication to teach her little ones the lessons she wished she had learned. While also making bedtime a little easier. The Queen, The Moon, and The Mountain is her debut work, dedicated to her daughter, Nyiema, and to every beautiful Black girl discovering the vastness of her greatness.